The Vigil

THE VIGIL

A POEM IN FOUR VOICES

Margaret Gibson

Louisiana State University Press / *Baton Rouge and London*

1993

Copyright © 1991, 1992, 1993 by Margaret Gibson
All rights reserved
Manufactured in the United States of America
First printing
02 01 00 99 98 97 96 95 94 93   5 4 3 2 1

Designer: Glynnis Phoebe
Typeface: Caslon Old Face #2
Typesetter: G & S Typesetters, Inc.
Printer and binder: Thomson-Shore, Inc.

Library of Congress Cataloging-in-Publication Data

Gibson, Margaret.
    The vigil / Margaret Gibson.
        p.   cm.
    ISBN 0-8071-1867-2. — ISBN 0-8071-1868-0 (pbk.)
    I. Title.
    PS3557.I1916V54   1993
    813'.54—dc20   93-12336
                                                        CIP

Portions of this book have appeared previously, sometimes in slightly different form, in *Indiana Review*, *Kentucky Poetry Review*, *Kestrel*, *Southern Review*, and *Tar River Poetry*, and in *Elvis in Oz: New Stories and Poems from the Hollins Creative Writing Program*, edited by Mary Campbell Flinn and George Garrett (University Press of Virginia, 1992).

All the characters in this volume are fictional, and any resemblance between them and anyone living or dead is entirely coincidental.

The paper in this book meets the guidelines for permanence and durability of the Committee on Production Guidelines for Book Longevity of the Council on Library Resources. ∞

For
Jacqueline, Ellen, Joanne, Marta, Stephanie,
Tina, Dana, Jeanne, and Flora

I want to thank the Connecticut Commission on the Arts for a grant that enabled me to begin work on this book. I am particularly grateful to Stephanie Strickland for her careful attention to *The Vigil* in manuscript as it evolved; to Joe Ellis, whose life, for himself and others, is a joyful renewal; and to Jack Troy, at whose anagama kiln in Huntingdon, Pennsylvania, I looked fire in the eye.

To the Reader

These are women's voices, each woman speaking to herself. There are four voices: Lila, Sarah, Jennie, Kate—mothers and daughters, three generations in a family shaped by, disrupted by alcoholism. Listening to them, we overhear the events of a single day in late October, 1986, when Sarah, a potter, holds a wood-kiln firing at her home in North Stonington, Connecticut—an annual vigil which draws the women in the family to Sarah's house to help out.

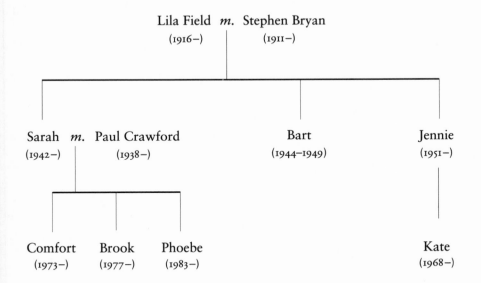

Lila Field *m.* Stephen Bryan
(1916–)   (1911–)

Sarah *m.* Paul Crawford   Bart   Jennie
(1942–)   (1938–)   (1944–1949)   (1951–)

Comfort   Brook   Phoebe   Kate
(1973–)   (1977–)   (1983–)   (1968–)

Sarah

From dreaming, I shudder awake—
hands open, no bowl
in my upturned palms, too warm
from the wood kiln,
the soughing of the fire
low, a taunt
if I want one to rouse me to work
I know I must do. I haven't kept
this vigil well enough.
I lift the kiln door
on its pulley—glowing chars,
wood scored by fire
to patterns that seem runic,
reticulate. Stacked plates
and stoneware jars shimmer,
pale in the red heat.
Cone four. The kiln's hung there.
I grab gloves and leather
apron—flame throwers, time
for that—and stack rough
slabs of oak
on the threshold, wood on a tilt
over embers, the atmosphere so hot
the wood, relumed, jets off

into the radiant moment of albedo, drawn
thirty feet inside, and surging.
I lift a bung—
fire billows where my face had been.
What's wrong—I don't know what,
but something, something's wrong.
Just dawn, but Kate's not here yet.
The apprentice potters haven't
come, and the work's meant
to be shared, communal.
Go downstairs and rest, last night
I told Lila—the weekend's meant
for joy as well as work—
any time now Kate
will be home. But not even my hand
put briefly against her cheek
could soften her scored frown.
Now muscle. Sweat and grit. One stoke
more, fire meets fire, and slowly
I relax into the solitude of the work
I love. Or I try,
then sink down on an empty pallet
to rest. I watch my hands tremble.
What's wrong—what have I done?

Cover it, cover it up, a wood thrush sings
in the shimmer of heat that rises
off the kiln. The kiln's tight
with ware, old forms I've outgrown—
and not a one of the new quite right.
Accept what unfolds as meant,
and be grateful—words I tell
to children. Are they false?
Today they feel false.
I look around. I'm alone—
and a sense
of forced work brings
me to a standstill, as tense
as Lila in the kitchen's yeasty
light. Something's wrong.
Something. And I don't know why.
I put my hands into a circle—
space turned and ringing,
so fully generous
it could hold sun and leaf,
field and Sound, house,
all my children safe.
I think of the empty space
that shapes a turning bowl—

my hands open, and the dream
returns to them, shimmering
whole. Again,
I fill a clear bowl
until it brims,
holding it steady in the sun.
The sea's far off, so small
I think I can pour it,
however infinite, roiling
into the bowl. *Where are you now?*
The dream shades into autumn
gardens, bare and black.
Before me the field turns
frost, the copper beech and maple
wine and flame.
Then first snow comes down,
brief and intricate,
a wet salt on my cheeks.
I watch each flake
melt into water and sun,
each pattern, each detail
dissolving—and now
nothing holds it back—
Someone's missing.

Trembling, the bowl deflects
light, slants it.
Into the dream, familiar hands appear,
pale hands,
almost transparent. I want
to cover these hands
with mine, to hold
until our hands fill with color—
somehow to atone within a matrix
of water and sun,
simple gifts. Is it enough,
this bowl? I offer it,
but the hands hold a hemisphere
of glass that matches with
mine rim for rim. I can
barely hear my own breath,
only stillness, only cold—
and finally, like a reflex
responsive to nothing
visible, nothing
heard in the dream, the hands put,
shining, the empty bowl over
mine, rim to rim—the sphere
turning in my hands.

Where are you now? I stoke
the primary air ports clean, air
eases in, coals
breathe. I breathe in, the dream fades
to a baffle of mist remembered
offshore in the Sound. First light
sifts up the wooded ridge
along field and pond.
It circles my house up the hill,
gathering earth and sky
around family and things
handed down, mother to daughter—
great-grandmother's prayer rug, its ocher
and Indian blue just right
for the kitchen. Our fine wood table,
round—even stones
picked up by the Sound, broken
glass washed soft by the sea,
books and notebooks,
the worn collar of the dog that died,
and our rings—things
to cherish and hold—
our lives like beads of mercury
that, touched, skid off fast as feeling.

Just like him to pick the wrong time,
last night I heard Jennie
mutter, alone with Lila in the kitchen
as I came in from seeing Paul off
to be with Father, flushed
with fever at the hospice, our children hushed
to sleep by stories—just the three
of us now together, not even
one night beneath the same roof—
and already I could feel
each of us pulled in, watchful.
As if an exacting angel
turned us inward, away from
whatever might be
said or done in truth, or pretense,
to soften grief
or give joy. Now this dream,
and no time for the relief
of working it into clay,
thinking only with my fingers, in a mime
transforming briefest glimpse
into work I can feel
on my pulse, into presence I can
shape and turn and, God help me, hold.

Lila

Hushabye,
                I remember whispering once,
mouth open and salty, Jennie curled
in my lap, close as a tendril,
Sarah's hands moving in practice,
a largo on the piano, notes she mutes
for my sake. Hush, he's gone.

And always I have let him go, glass
by glass, and let him,
returning, move us, move me
from one gilded house to another,
following his blueprints
and the luck of the drawing board.
So much luck—you are central
to my success, he said. *Hushabye,*
I remember whispering.

Round, around the walnut table
with its central stem and lion's feet
(where the children, barefoot, put
their toes in the smooth grooves
and stroked the beast beneath the table)
I gathered us for dinners.
I remember an idle talk of boats
and houses, tall glasses of iced tea,
cups of milk. I remember how Stephen
carved, each slice so perfectly
drawn down he might as well have used
his architect's rule. I remember
linens that were never marked
by purpled circles or half circles.
Bart sailed bread cubes
over the surface of his soup. Sarah made

stories from her blue willow plate—
birds changed back to lovers,
a house floated like a flower
beneath a bridge, around the world
to China, where someone needed succor,
needed her potatoes—I'd given
her too much to eat.

I remember Stephen missing dinner—
too much work, late conferences, too much
booze—each absence so unpredictable
I refused to take out a table leaf
or know he wasn't coming. I liked
our dinner mats just to touch
at the top corners. I liked the easy
reach of hands joined first
to bless this food to our use,
the easy reach of my fork into Sarah's
plate, into Bart's.
                    I remember, oh,
setting the table the night
Bart died, four places, and his special
cup—I had to, I don't know why.
Although Stephen, pushing his plate
into the flowers, scraping the floor
with his chair, said he knew.
Sarah watched us dry eyed.
Her spoon turned circles in her soup.
The ripples widened, and when
Jennie came to be in Bart's place,
the emptiness filled. We were
a happy family, or I wanted us
to be. I remember learning to say,
Just finish your drink in the study,

Stephen, we'll start. And he might
come in by dessert with his blueprints
and word games, and bourbon was Lipton's,
water gin, and Jennie
went angrily off to her room
where I'd gather her, or I'd send food
up by Sarah. I remember firing the cook.
I remember refusing to shop, taking
meals out when Sarah left for college
and Jennie had sports, leaving him
alone, wherever he was by then,
home or not, delicately rigged
inside the glass of a bottle, a schooner
moored on air.

And now again he's betrayed us! breaking
years of careful silence as you'd break
glass, unraveling the family
to its very root, telling his beloved,
his granddaughter, his Kate,
what we'd kept from her.

And still Sarah doesn't know, moving
in darkness as if it were her own
familiar light. *Don't tell her
yet*, Jennie said. *I'll tell her.*
And so I have only myself to talk to—
up early, sacrificed, and guilty—
setting the kettle, water over fire.
Setting out flour, yeast. Honey, salt.
Making bread for the feast that follows
Sarah's firing, her kiln burning
night and day—bowls and pots,
six months' work, hers

and the other women's work stacked
carefully in the kiln, whose slow
first fires she started, alone, last night.
Since midnight she's been down there
in her long leather apron, slowly stoking.
Give Sarah time, Jennie said. *Kate
has the rest of her life, now, to know.*

He said he would build me a house
I could live in forever—
he said that, holding tightly to my arm,
and the summer sound
that rises from dry grasses filled my ears.

And now, neither the play of light on
the glaze of a bowl nor light
breaking into the field
nor the simple work of kitchen ritual
keeps it back—

Oh I can't, I won't—

forgive him.

Sarah

I stoke more wood, I stack
more stubborn wood, until a quick
scrape of one knuckle,
and some blood,
so slight a pain, bring back
the dream's transparent hands.
They hold me still as I work.
I've seen them before.
Fire rises in the kiln, rhythmic,
like the sea—and I know
them—pale
hands, like sea glass—now
a childhood
morning, the early dream I called
Angel, unfolding—those hands, numinous
in my open window, sun on the sill,
wind luffing the curtain. And no one
there to tell me what I felt
pressing, unspoken.
I woke. The sun lit my window,
lit the surface of the Sound outside
to a field of broken glass.
Just as the rope of an anchor,
entering water, seems bent,

my father's there on the grass,
bent over, refracted, in silhouette—
my father against the open sky
and broken sea,
crying out for anyone to come,
and when no one comes, he moves slowly
toward the sleeping house.
Closer, I see against his shirt
the small body, folded—head
down, Bart—he brought
Bart inside
and tucked him, fully dead,
back into the cooled, rumpled
sheets he'd snuck from.
I watched from the door,
keeping still, as my father
sat there and sat there
on the edge of the small bed
weeping, unaware
of the luminous circle that rippled
around them both, my brother
quiet, too quiet
in the turning light—
and then my mother, voice hoarse

in accusation, now shrill,
her fear translated into curt
rhythmic beats—*your* fault,
your fault—the words
flung home by my mother's fist
frantic on the air
as he sat there, at a standstill,
his face turned away,
the light I'd seen gathering
calmly, like water in water
or air in air, retreating,
the power of the dark
for the moment ascending—
the only sign he knew anyone there
in the room a faint shudder
as he took, too quietly,
her word, his guilt—
his home-late, late-night, blacked-out
guilt—to heart. He'd left the door
unlocked, hadn't he?—words
that I, by the door, keeping still
in the spent light, knew to be
stones hurled blindly,
unjustly, though they hit their mark.

Stunned, like my father,
I turned away as my mother
took Bart's head to her breast,
and rocked him, and rocked him.
I turned away—how could I have held
that image before me and not felt
him gone, fully gone?
Couldn't he just sleep? the wet
on my mother's gown
just milk—not this madness,
cold and salty. Had I told the truth . . .
I unlocked it . . .
(two hands on the knob, both
needed to pull the door open,
chill air sliding in, and his car,
dim as a ship on the hazard
of the sea, safe, home).
Had I told them
my ritual—how I'd leave bed
to see the light beneath
their door, then (magically) spread
light through the dark house
just by thinking it.
But I saw the curtain fill with breath,

morning wind, and I called it
Angel—as if it were life force,
and I was lifted
by a secret trust—*Tell no one.*
And those words, risen
through me like light—
I trusted them, without
knowing why—*Tell no one.*
I might have disobeyed,
done something, said . . .
but I held in my breath,
complicit, afraid—
watching as their anger turned
in me, invisibly,
to guilt. No one
to turn to. Only wind, and those
hands, pale as glass,
that seemed to herald loss,
then fade to tangible emptiness.
I was willing to let truth
do its own work, without me.
Willing to lie,
to wait, doing nothing that would
risk loss

of their love. I turned away
into my own life. But something
to touch—I needed that.
Need that. I hold,
a moment longer,
Bart's body,
cradled in wood grain and sun,
body of light—then rouse
myself, raise
the kiln door, feed
wood to the coals. In the flare
of fire here I am, still spreading
light through the house,
just by thinking it.
I shake my head. The light cannot
reach to my father,
left far on the family's cold
circumference, in the hospice
failing and alone. And where's Kate?
The day's practice begins—I need
patience, a brimming
bowl in which to carry light
safe, whole. The day will turn.
The pattern holds. *Tell no one.*

Jennie

Quicksilver, top-speed, invisible in a rush of wind—just feel it! Nothing holds me. Over ocean and inlet, now I see the fields below me stretch out: familiar: muscular and rolling: mown rows, curved lines so fluent, they remind me of women's voices: in the background Lila's voice, or Sarah's, or Kate's. Whose filmscript is this? In the field the rows coil, they darken and revolve, a storm held low to the earth, a clock of winds pressed down into sod. A sudden shift: sun rises in another dream. A woman goes barefoot in an alley of litterings and abortions, stainless steels and glass and foils and plastics. The city inhabits her, a cry of ashes, ashes, all fall down— brief houses, black skyscrapers, all fall down. My dreaming tumbles: head over heels: into a gasp of giggles, into a wriggle in the covers like a kitten after anything that moves, into a boy—this small boy crying, *Wake up, Aunt Jennie, wake up!*

And it's not my room, mine in New York with my books and papers, proof
sheets, cameras. There, blown inward, the curtains belly out in the press of
city wind, city smell, city street noise. In my kitchen, an icebox: a hot
plate: a sink that serves to rinse pasta, rinse fresh fruit, wash the body.
Away now from that oasis of work and my own spare needs, I wake here:
in Sarah's house: in a boy's room, the weight of the moment felt as eighty
pounds, pure boy. Brook wears a jay's blue feather held fast beneath the
Velcro of the red right shoe. He brings cinnamon toast, homemade, yeasty—
Gramma's gift, he says, her offhand voice turned perfectly in his throat.
Then in a whisper, furtive: *Get dressed. I've got something to show you out-
side!* I grumble, a show of resistance he thinks is funny. Over my head, on
the kitchen's clay tiles, Lila's footsteps, tapping. Sun floods the bed, too
bright. A mobile of silver sailboats turns and turns. The pond's eye flashes.
Out there, hoarfrost, woodsmoke, wind. Out there: far: Kate unfurls a sail
that fills with salt: with distance. Sarah's working. Our father's dying. It's
a plot.

Hide the toast: beneath the papers on the desk. I remember, *Go to your room*—that cherished command, and he'd furl open blueprints of a new house he'd designed, running his tongue over his teeth: a taste of ice and olives. Back then, it was *Go to your room*, argue with the mirror, never take his part unless to spy out weakness, then write the words down: write them down. Better that than the walls of clearest gin he would raise around him in the afternoons they called my childhood: each afternoon early night-fall, even in summer. *Go to your room*. Outside this room Brook insists his body into the crack of the door, a silent urgency, *Please hurry*. As I dress, I hear the echo in my head, my own voice answering the voice in the door, *I'm coming*. And I laugh. I'm actually glad to, pulling on the heaviest wool I have as we fly off: conspirators: no good-mornings to anyone upstairs: out the side door, down the sloped hill, on to the yellow leaves of the fire road, into the trees.

He takes me over slouches of wall, through yellow fern, through hooks
that lash to my wool. I'm no more right for this scrambling than my shoes
are. I don't look to see what he's pointing at: can't afford to: not until I get
there, solid earth underfoot. I leap, land upright, hand on the root—the
root?—for that's what this coil is, a knot of root upended into air when the
tree blew down. The tree still flourishes, a portion of the root uprisen, the
long trunk level with the brook. On it two branches have risen steeply to-
ward the light: slim, straight trees. Between these, a tree house whose walls
are wind. My small godchild's already up there, grinning. But I'm held
here: hand on the thick ring of root: dark coils from the field of the dream—
here the dream is. Joined to the trunk of the blow-down. What is this I'm
feeling? Here is the brook that feeds the Indian Swamp, that feeds the
Mystic River, that feeds into the Sound, that floats under the boat Kate sails
on. The word seeps out: *afraid*.

My hand's on the root. The root's out of the soil, turned out, its coils branching, round and round. I remember the childhood I lived, the other I wished for. In one childhood, my father's a drunk. In the other, he's not. In one, the ocean is gin. In the other, water. In the world whose ocean is gin, whose sun is beer, betrayal is a daily fact. The father drinks. The father denies that he drinks. The mother wipes up spills, bakes bread, and takes him back. In the world of spills and lies, there are two sisters: they both want the other world, whose ocean is water. Sarah sees things and touches them: sees and touches, both at once. The years go by. A young man burns his draft card, blurs over the border, into Canada. Even at a distance, Sarah sees a dark-haired child, picks up the phone, as if there were no distance, no lies, no line between sleeping and waking, no separate worlds. And yes, I say: *I am pregnant*. The universe splits into *is* and *isn't*. In one world, confined, I give birth, and there's Kate. For the sake of the new child, we agree to secrets we don't want. Now I'm the aunt who rarely visits, feeling odd. I see Kate, the child who is: who isn't: mine. Sarah is the mother: and isn't. But in the world I renounced: in the world with no birth: none: I live with a sound as small as the slosh of gin in a tumbler. The sound turns into water: only water I lie: and the tiny embryo in blood sloshes out, a sucking sound. Then a world of breathless silence, all secrets kept.

In this world of roots and blow-downs, shoes wet, feet cold, stalled on the rung of the ladder: here I am, led out of myself by the mute beseeching in this small boy's eyes. I climb the ladder slowly, giving in to how I imagine Sarah's life to be. *What goes on up here?*—my tone light as a leaf, expecting blood ritual: bonding: a tree-house rite, the plot that pulls the outsider in: you're one of us, you're mine. He whispers, *If you sit still, when the deer come, they won't see you, and they'll stay.* I nod, he's very serious. We sit quietly together. Freeze frame: projecting myself off the platform to the border of the brook, looking back at myself: close up. But Brook looks around for deer to come into the clearing lit by sun. We sit and wait—I've been waiting: all these years: for the bad news that claps like thunder: the opposite of applause. The reel rewinds—again I open the letter: read it: slip the words back between the torn lip of the envelope. A blur of pain comes first. *Dear Mother . . .* Then a blur of relief: get used to the feel of it: never mind your mind. *I underline the words out of my disbelief, to make myself believe. My hand is shaking as I write. Dear Mother . . .*

Back then my choice was self and school and work on public issue. Da Nang, Can Tho, My Lai, Ben Tre. *We had to destroy it in order to save it.* Never mind the Perfume River, the graceful green pagodas, Hue. Along the avenues dead bodies stink. A child requires your attention? Never mind the secret bombings, the blood. Be blind to the twisting cartwheels of the albatross, air on fire with radiation, Christmas Island. Never mind. You've come a long way (*baby*, the word is still *baby*)—watch the backlash. A child requires your attention. Never mind the caste system of sex, the arms race, the husbandmen. For an absolute weapon, an absolute enemy's required. Never mind fallout, rainout, snowout: *the chafe and jar of nuclear war:* the mottled necrosis of what's left of woods and fields. Never mind as the world burns and turns: the tacky filmscript: *A Blissful Reunion of a Lost Mother and Her Child.* Remember: *I look into the air and find the spaces where our children might be.* Remember: *Shall there be womanly times, or shall we die?* I did not choose to live in this time. And I did not choose these words, *Dear Mother . . .*

Dear Mother, if I have two mothers, you sometimes have been my favorite. You fight your way, you do what you want. Should I come live with you? Would you want me? Brook nudges closer, and I keep my body still: there for him: no shifting of my body away from his. What does he know: really know: about anyone in the family? Grown-ups are simple shelters to nudge into. I shiver. *Dear Mother, Grampa talks to himself when he drinks, looks into the window glass and talks. One night I listened.* The letter falls to the kitchen table. The letter falls to the table, and Lila's hand touches my sleeve. Lila's face, reflected on the dark window glass, opens into the NO of pain that can't be said to anyone. Stephen told her? NO. In that mirror we both turn away. I watch as I pull away from her body, from her offer of simple comfort—that offer never simple. A mother needs to comfort: to stand still in that power: just as she wants for her own self some small comfort: the touch of her hand on an arm that won't pull away.

Water breaking over stone. The running brook brings back the sound of bath water sponged down my neck: over my back and shoulders: over my belly, and my mother kneeling beside the wide tub, or in the water with me, the innocence of that water splashing both our skins, the slippery shine of soap on my mother's breasts. One day, mine would change from two brown pennies: my father called them two brown pennies: to the soft-slung, eloquent gravity of my mother's breasts: *jackpots* he called them: outsider: standing there in the bathroom door, looking on. Back then, I wasn't allowed to draw my bath or bathe alone. Whenever I wanted to walk to the dock, to swim, I had to wait for Sarah. *Be careful, be like me,* my mother's daily life instructed, though the words rhymed in my head with the unspoken: *Don't be*—a fear that felt like Bart's room: Don't touch: secret: don't touch. Don't touch, don't speak. And we never spoke of him: my brother: the boy before my birth: his existence a figment from which we turned in silence: away.

There! Brook whispers. I turn abruptly. The deer startles, turns tail, runs. The white flash rises and falls like the curl of a wave over tree stumps and stone walls, into the closed yellow wood. I'm sorry I moved so fast, I want to say so—but Brook is excited by the white flash of the deer through the woods. *At least you saw it a little,* he whispers. *That counts.* I don't know what counts and what doesn't, but I'm glad he's glad I've seen. Now we're free to go down the ladder slowly, across the water of the brook, slowly home. Brook gathers the yellow leaves into a handful, like flowers. We will give them to Sarah, I'll turn from the color of my fear, and I'll tell her, *Kate's not coming home.* The woods are yellow, the whole world is burning yellow. Smoke rises from the kiln shed—black, then gray, then white. A car's pulling in: the other potters. And there's Sarah. My heart rises in my throat. *Dear Mother, I can't come home just yet. You go tell Mom—tell Sarah—what Grampa said. I haven't got the heart to yet.*

Kate

Never mind, I keep telling myself. *You can't be. You're not.*

I sling on my knapsack, tide fills my footprints, I'm gone,
moving fast over sea-foam and pebble, oar weed and dulse,

devil's apron, wrack and shell. I wheel to a stop,
unpeeling knapsack, sweater, camisole, and shirt. Left bare,

betrayed by everyone, here I am, by God—nerve and skin.

I want to feel wind, wind only, fit me. New wind drives over
the water, wrinkling its cold blue silk. The wind

turns me. Trues me. Nothing that lies can touch me here.

Tick tick tick is the bird in the beach plum.
Uh uh uhh is the fleet shade of bird flying over wet sand.

Farther out, two loons skim the surface, slicing into the blade
of the horizon swiftly. *Choose what is light,*

Sarah said once. *There is pattern and sign,* she said,
a guidance of the spirit.

But, looking into horizon, into nothing, where the loons went,
I see nothing sacred. At my feet, a shell with chamfered

wings hinged wide, the damp mass, the clot of clay that, raw,
made me gag—gone, the inside a rinsed milk blue.

I snap and fling it back into the slur of mussels a tide of gulls
churned and picked clean. *Ah-eee* is the sea horn,

ah-eee is the sea, unmothering. What else can I do?

Wind roughs my hair. In the wind I hear Daniel, his tongue
wet in my ear, whispering earthquake, avalanche, hurried words

about order in chaos, multifractal or fractal, all the while
inside my sweater, one hand tensing my nipple, the other

down the small of my back, inside my jeans, his fingers fragrant
with me, bringing the smell of me into the hollows of my neck

and collarbone, into my navel. Just a touch, inside, his words
a flow of wind across bare skin. Not need not anger not love

and not just sex, this front flowing through me, ellipsoidal
(he said), kin to eddies of grain, kin to light that flickers

from quasars, cone by cone kin to the escalade of fire
inside a kiln. But I'm alone. Fact?

Fact. Daniel said so. *The Petrel* is docking for winter.
I have nowhere to go.

On *The Petrel*, into the last hours of my watch, into a soft
seaway of fog, a low breathing came. No wind,

no wind on the mirrory sea floor. Into that calm sea room
broke a bird, osprey or gull, then a pale coil of silver,

the sun, buzzed and weird, seared my name, sealed my name

into everything misted around me—sun bird boat
all Kate, all a halyard hitch fouled, a wheel that won't

center or true—and no influx of music or books, no spin
of the counterclockwise wheel makes sweet

the spoiled work. I'm what they made me,

our whole family architects of the expendable,
objects that dunt, unravel, rive, capsize, or muddle.

And no matter what I do, or say, I can't make this body
obey me, mind, or say clearly what Daniel said, meanly—

You're not pregnant, that old trick, that lie.

Lila

I brood on the pond, its skim of ice
now melting—listening
to the migrant yelp of geese flying over.
There once, naked and sturdy, young Kate
scooped the shallows, her fingers
intent on birds that flew along
in the sky of the water.
As she moved, I moved—felt
water rising up my thigh,
felt cold water closing on my sex—
then a flutter, feathery, across my fingers—
almost! almost alive in my granddaughter's
body, her lithe skin mine,
no distance or lies, no line between us.

But here's a flutter of yellow—Brook
racing uphill from the pond,
impossible child, and I can feel it—
he'll get hurt, too quick
for them, busy with their wood and fire
and clay talk—he'll get hurt,
only four years older than Bart was.
And now comes Jennie,
striding across grass and gravel,
straight toward Sarah, a burden to dispatch,
make no mistake—and Sarah turns
toward her, smiles, and they embrace.
Arms around each other, each steps back,
enough space for a steady look
and words, a hum of them. My breath
sucks in, muscles tighten—
they are standing on the dock at home,
in Stonington, younger—and Stephen

is ill—I'm alone, they will
leave me with him.
                        Once, so young, a child,
I came into the room where my mother lay
too ill to know me. The distance
illness put between us I couldn't cross,
nor ask her to say, *I love you.*
She said it in the ring she left me after
she died, ring I turned round and round,
too large an emptiness for any finger
on my small hand then. And I saved
that ring for Sarah—for my first daughter,
I said, when she gives me a granddaughter.

I close my eyes and see a room
so white that, drawn there,
I can almost touch Stephen's loneliness.
I let my hands slide slowly down
the soft folds of my neck
and come to rest on my breasts,
on my belly.
                        I remember the black dress,
silk I wore at the service for Bart—
as faded now as the flower I pinned
to the smooth coil I made of my hair—
quiet, so quiet as a murmur of friends
ringed us, remembering Bart.
Silent, Stephen nodded, and looked away.
Sarah was to save us, Sarah was to play
the sonata she was too young for.
I remember her hands hovering over
the keys, not about to let anyone down.
She would stir these strangers to applause,
redeem her mother, forgive her father—

how we trusted her gift! her calm,
her poise. She was a perfect daughter,
glad to please—never mind
(she told me later) how clumsy she felt,
how wretched, how wrong.
Oh, but how could you, golden child, my
jonquil, be wrong? She looked at me
as if I were a hill far away.
Then she smiled, her skin going pale.

Sarah

I stand still. I stand still
in a windy light that lifts
smoke from the kiln.
The shaking in me
settles. I am calmer. Calm.
Kate's not coming home.
I wheel around toward
the kiln. But the others have come.
Brook's playing by the shelf
of unfired pots. I have shifts
to assign, and soon, oh God—
I turn back toward the pond.
What does this feel
like?—too much sand
in a clay that rasps and smarts
against my palm as the wheel
spins. My eyes sting. I try
to center. Whatever Jennie said,
I struggle not to feel.
But my eyes fill. The world
around me blurs, unsafe.
Kate's not coming home—
she doesn't want to see me,
she's gone off—angry,

and I am stone
sinking down beneath a surface
blown to ripples by bright wind,
stone sinking down
past a slither of milt
and leaf mold, past wavering weeds,
stone settling down in a mud
of muck, cold silt, and root.
I swallow hard.
Kate knows, and I must
find her, hold her.
But someone calls out a question—
there's work at hand,
this rush of fire and air
that allows us
only a brief illusion of control,
and that barely. A friend
feels my tension—
something's wrong?—her hand gentle
on my arm. I only nod
and go with her. Rachel. My apprentice.
I'm in charge—but all the while
as we sidestoke and check the cones
in the back, where the ware

is stacked tight, I'm elsewhere,
stone in deep water,
wondering, what does this feel like?
I sidestoke—where is Brook?
Stacking planks. In one
I see a nail—*Watch out!*
I yell, so intense
he looks away, hopping on one foot,
playful, pretending nonchalance.
I let him be, carrying oak
to the kiln, and the rhythm of the work,
stacking and unstacking
wood as we stoke,
nearly lulls me. Oh, but where
was I when he told her—
dreaming? turning
my father's (soon, own) urn
on the wheel? in a trance of diligence
making things? feeling the unspoken
stir and strain
to rise only in the pause between
the turn, and turn
again, of clay to make a cup another
might drink from? And look

what I have let happen!
I lift a bung—a flume of fire,
pale gold, a river
rush of it, sweeps over the ware.
My eyes come to rest on
the urn I made for my father,
like a Sung
vase or a soul on fire
cleanly given form. How the fire
burns it! urn of my stillborn
anger—a capacity
to forget what, long
ago, I knew—
I must change my life. Jaw
rigid, breath shallow, tongue dry—
and now Rachel, her hand on my arm,
draws me away
from any pretense of authority
or control. Dear God, I pray,
don't let me translate
what I feel into overt
act, grief or blame,
not that, not now.
But the words are coming out, *It's Kate,*

she's gone off . . . she's found out . . . ,
but how can I say it?
All the world, all my children
think Kate's mine,
my daughter. *She's found out . . . ,*
I repeat, stumbling, as Rachel,
thrown by my loss of composure,
wildly guesses, *She's pregnant?*
I shake my head *no,*
but her words fall like a blow,
glancing on my heart.
Something tells me she's right—
right, but premature.
I shouldn't have to know
this, now—
her words a portent
of more troubles hell-bent
in coming. Or am I mistaken,
wrong? All day long, all night
hasn't everyone known more
than I, obscure
in my private lament for my father,
for Bart—when all the while
in the guile of dream I've known

someone's missing. *Cover for me—just
this while,* I ask Rachel
and sit down on a bench before
the fire door, letting body
sink into memory,
into the drug of memory—
shielded by years
and a leather apron. But still,
pain—pain
licks my throat dry,
burns and presses, so tense
an anger it could rekindle
fire from ash. Irrelevant as dust,
words—*vincristine, oncovin*—
worry their way
back. Again I am in med school
deliberately failing. I can't work.
I can't make
work matter, despite the evidence
of my brilliant first year.
Why won't they see
what's wrong—I can't feel my body,
neither the joy of sleep or food, nor
the more vivid rushing of desire.

I could feel only my father's anger—
I was not, as I was,
enough—and never would be.
I study coals raked out the port,
the seeds of light within them slowly
winking out—I was like *that*.
I breathe in hard, until I feel the pulse
in my gut. In my gut
I remember the accident—my car
turning over, the road wet,
broken windshield glass
splayed out on tarmac. A red whir.
Then in a white room, voices.
I had broken my pelvis—
I might never have children—
and it comes together now, one cry
rising from my gut, a cry
for the woman I was then
met in my throat by one
for Kate—for, meaning to love her,
what have I done?
Another cry—
it's Brook, it's Brook hurt,
I run to him, our voices one voice, hurt.

Jennie

The garden's black from the killing frost, only parsley left green and spriggy. Up the hill, the house our father planned, Sarah's house, fits the contour of the hill, an outcropping of wood and stone among tall trees. I remember the whir of my camera: subversive: the camera Paul won't allow me to bring to this house: not ever again: I'm reshooting the opening frames of *Sarah's House*. I'm twenty-eight again: not loved enough, and restless. The camera tracks uphill, the camera circles the house, the camera is prodigal sister, she who comes too late, the straggler. The camera prowls the rooms, recording the particular silence of these walls and sofas, rugs and tables, fire screen, bowls and windows: and outside there is wind—feel the wind!—pure movement that, restless, is going, going, never in one place long: long gone: the wind flowing over everything equally. The camera sifts and separates, seizes and excludes. The family doesn't see, but the eye of the camera turns toward the family blind spot. I decide on silence. *No words: I will privilege the wind.* Beyond the boundaries of Sarah's bowls, beyond Sarah's house and Sarah's face: beyond even the rim of the isolating wind that circles and circles the house, they do not hear the cries that whirl and mount: outside: denied.

The camera circles the house. In the world Sarah's willed, the garden grows heavy, the chickens scratch in the yard for worms, the far owl hoos. The wheel turns: the pond's eye flashes, the husband comes home. She scrubs potatoes, stirs soup. She rinses her hands in water she once dowsed for. The Haitian cleaning woman comes. The children cry. The husband leaves for the hospital to work. No sound but wind: then, closeup: Sarah: her face as the wheel turns, slow. Her face as she lifts a sweater from the floor and folds it. Her face as the plates fill and empty. Her face and the color of fire on her face as she waits for her husband: a face turned inward, no sound but wind—then gradually riding on the wind, the cries of women: in Viet Nam, the villages: in Laos, the Plain of Jars: in El Salvador, in Buenos Aires: *las madres*. No sound but wind: then the sound of strafing, street cries, a swell of siren, and slowly the house on the screen dissolves, and Sarah's face fades: white: bone white: and the cries of invisible women (elsewhere, desperate) fill the screen, which is dark now, empty: no sound but wind.

There is nothing wrong here: don't tell anyone. Last night: in the kitchen windows: I saw myself come in on Lila and Phoebe shaking a jar of cream, passing it back and forth between them, making butter. Not loved enough: restless: I watched myself watch them. I felt sudden pain: I saw the home window, in Stonington, dark. I saw my father. I saw my hand wet with wine pick glasses by stem or rim from the table—the guests aghast, my father roaring—and fling them, glass and wine, on the tile floor in the candlelight: broken lights. I'm barefoot. I can do this, I think in the whirl and mount of anger: and this, as I toss the last of the wine at the window, just the wine, which drips down the panes where surely Lila must have been able to see: reflected: his hand wander out of sight, under the table, into the blind spot: wandering.

We were in the kitchen. In full view of her guests: a magician: Lila cooked at the burnished stove, a dash of wine and spices—some stylish sauté. Linen and silver, flowers, French peasant plates. Guests. These decent, these dangerous people. The conversation rambled: voices I kept in the background: genial voices: disturbed: what to do to win in Viet Nam. My father poured wine. I was put across from him at the narrow trestle table, next to a woman whose face even then was a blur. *And she had so many gifts*, I hear Lila say of Sarah, rueful. Sarah: first daughter destined to achieve, who'd left music for medicine, medicine for clay and a wheel somewhere in the sticks outside Charlottesville, where—Stephen interrupts, *Next thing you know, she'll take a lover.* I grin. The face beside me responds in wine and laughter at my father's caustic wit. We're at dinner in the kitchen: *en famille.*

Just then: in sharper focus: for me: for me only: a child screams down the napalmed road, a child in searing motion. I can see her. The girl's dress and the flames billow out, dress and flame full—she is running wing and wing. No one else sees her. Just as no one sees in the windows of the dark French doors my father's hand beneath the table: my father too drunk to know my thigh from hers across the table: his hand in the folds of my skirt, wandering. *At least now she's married,* I hear Lila say: just then: I rise with the first glass in hand: startled: his: his glass in my hand: and I'm knocking my chair back as I rise, I am one swift motion.

I am free of them: I thought that: my foot cut and bleeding. Free of him, standing outside on the cold grass. But in the morning, there was quiet: a truce, as after one of my father's binges. No one made inquiry: no one overtly blamed. No one explained, apologized. My father made breakfast, frowning: glad to serve. He stood chilled, remote, remorseful. Lila asked about my homework. She glanced at the cut on my instep, still raw. Cease-fire—or better, no-fire: as if nothing had happened. And indeed nothing had. Denied, the moment would repeat itself, a pattern. Looking back, I see glass broken, a good wine spilled, a clean floor swept clean. Looking back, I hear words fly off into wind, my father's drunk talk. I hear words hushed in the marrow of my mother's bones. Looking back, through the window I see them settle back to the table and serve the sherried veal, gone cold. In the background: Lila's voice: a whisper: *That high-rise, collapsing; her father's lawsuit pending; and the pressure from colleges: so many interviews, so little sleep.*

Kate

I pull off my jeans and touch where I cleave inward. No sign,
no smear, bright or rusty.

When Sarah touches clay, it opens like a tulip, her left hand
deep in the whorl of the clay, lifting that dark

inner space, that night sky, curving it gently, her right hand
on the outside horizon, steady,

as the clay thins and thins, rising to its singular rim,
that edge where *I am* meets *I am not.*

I squint at the sun, hot fire hung over sea and riprap wall,
this far bell marking the shoal off Napatree.

I'm firing my own clay in the sun, and the sun's solid gold,
an old rock-and-roll hit blasting loud as a jukebox.

I'm this body reduced to bare essence and glaze,

just a kid on the beach. *She's too old to take off her shirt,*
Gramma fusses, and off goes also Grampa's,

just to spite her. I can tell Grampa's drunk—the vein on
Gramma's temple throbs. *Black gum against thunder,* she says

as he visits his dopkit again, and the flask flashes silver.
Then oil in the palm of his hand smoothes over my shoulders,

around the nip of my neck, down my arms, his hands flying fast
up my belly, over xylophone, collarbone,

up and over, slipping the oil on as you'd slip off a shirt.

The vein on Gramma's temple throbs, but he's teaching me solids
and cavities, the wet sand tricked by his hand

into pediment and gable. Santa Maria della Pace. A campanile.
Santa Andrea della Fratte. Cantilevers that jut out

and fall, della Splatte. Cave temples of India, castles,
room raum rum, build anything you want, *There's room.*

Grampa fell. Not a long fall, just over the rim of concrete
in the parking lot, the yachts bobbing,

a soft landing in the salt of the marina he called *margarita*
when he laughed with the waitress in the *tea room,*

his trousers making puddles on the floor. Gramma studied a pastel
on the wall, its monkey putting apricots back in a bowl,

not a single one let to fall over the rim, out the frame,
to the floor. Home, I watched my father's jaw

grow rigid. Mom said, *No more in the car with Grampa,*
no more castles. *Your Grampa's spoiled,* like the apricots,

had they fallen to the floor, like some children, *spoiled,*
she said, withdrawing. But I loved him.

Help this poor old body to die, said Grampa,

muzzy and fuddled, passing the buck down the bloodline.
So I took him wine, sneaking it past the nurses, a red claret

stowed in a duffle bag deep enough to house a jib. *Ah, now
it's spring, earth flows with the nectar of bees,*

he said, mocking his thirst, celebrating its power,
more than physical. But he was small in his bed as a boy.

No pity, he shot back at me. *No one knows, really knows,
what a body's for.*

Lila

A fly buzzes, autumn fat, on the sill.
I put out butter to soften.
A jar of honey, hive round.
I can ready the terra cotta pot for tea—
someone's cold hands will need
to clasp a warm cup. I can
let water, drawn from dark to light,
up Sarah's well, fill the kettle,
letting water run over my hand,
down the tips of my fingers—
water can spurt from my fingers,
charged with clear will—
what's left to me of God mumbled
in the old prayer—*Let me walk
into the works prepared for me*—
and if my work be absence,
well then, let me feel what a presence
absence is, let it suck my breasts,
let it turn in bed beside me, let it
hover on the unstruck keys of the piano
I abandoned to raise my children.

Downstairs, a run of seven notes,
a pause. I live in the pause. Seven more.
Comfort's plying away at her cello.
More scales, minor—a change of key
and even so, with music halting,
with water flowing, I hear the door
click open, and I startle, turning
quickly—Sarah, it will be Sarah,
who will tell me . . . but no—Jennie,
with a thick bouquet of parsley,
more than anyone can use, held stiffly
out before her. I want to laugh—

nearly do, she reminds me so of a small
boy, his frilly valentine carried
before him, green shield in the lush
fields of love, or love rejected.
But laugh? I cannot.
I swallow hard and reach for a glass,
the first I can find, a glass snifter
Sarah uses for flowers, and I fill it
with water quickly—just turning
in time, afraid I'll do something
(so small a thing, anything) wrong.

I hardly breathe. *In here,* I say.
Downstairs the cello smoothes a ragged phrase,
and Jennie tucks the parsley
into the globe of glass,
so close to me her breath
mingles with mine, I smell the cold air
on her clothes, a musk of mud on her shoes.
Ah, but our hands never touch—
we must want it that way.
Done, she replies. We smile—
but we don't mean it—and the world's
led back from chaos, fresh and green.

Then the door's flung open, hard—
and in Sarah hurries,
Brook scooped in her arms and crying—
crying—
            and I'm thrusting (I see myself
thrusting) the globe of parsley toward Jennie,
rushing past her (*This could happen,
I said so*) crying,
                    Angel, Angel! Oh, no.

Jennie

Her cry cleaves the air. I'm brushed by her breasts as she stumbles on the rug and hurries past. Water spills. Stalks of parsley fall, pell-mell at my feet. I don't know what to do with a hurt child. I hear Lila breathing, breathless. I hear Sarah send her usefully downstairs for salve as she sinks down on the sofa with Brook, who whimpers. His arm is burned. I hear a cello pause, and in the pause between two notes, the mask of fear on Brook's face tightens, his body the long shudder that cries, *Don't touch me, don't leave me, touch me.* That pain: it's as tangible as my body. I'm looking for someone to blame. Lila's luckier—how her hands must be moving! frantic in the chest of medicines downstairs. But, *Here you are, Angel. Here you are.* She's back upstairs, watching Sarah, watching Sarah's hands: like wings: move through the air above Brook's body, not touching him: her hair spilling forward, body intent, hands smoothing the air, hands stroking the air, as if air were a lover's body, a body her hands know, and know well. And Brook, the muscles in his face are softening, the mask of his fear dissolving. He is water: she is wing and wing on the wind.

Lila

I move nearer, but not too near.
I know better than to break the spell
between a mother and her child. I know
too well a bright trust, wounded.
Sunder and give, now the great dark
gapes—I am holding Bart
against my breast, wet and cold.
I wanted to hum a song—my son
loved a song before he slept—
but, angry at his father, stunned
and torn, I said, *Go on,*
go to her, the one you were with
last night. Over her son,
Sarah's hands gently move,
like leaves swept along by wind
above a broken surface—
and in one motion the fire
that burned and the burned flesh
gather, also sun and wind,
the smell of bread, Jennie's frank
dismay, and my fear—
whatever in pain is isolate
and torn, she gathers.
I feel my hands want to rise,
want to move with hers—oh, but
I couldn't do that! Not now, now then.
I held, and I hold, his cold body
to my breast, a bright trust
wounded. I remember how Sarah,
on her own, fetched a neighbor. How Stephen
fled upstairs. How the useless doctor
stood there, cajoling. I let my son
be taken from me. I let him sleep
without a song from my lips. I let

a stranger's hands take and probe,
undress, and (finally) dress him
for his final sleep. I lay in bed
that night, imagining

                    my hands were
with him. I starched the shirt.
I pressed his trousers.
I parted and combed his bright hair,
letting the cowlick (even then)
have its will. I laced his polished
shoes, I crossed his hands,
I sat with him. I couldn't sing,
but I saw it through to dawn.
I shut the coffin then, the sun
too bright. From my bed in the dark,
so alone,
           I did this.

Sarah

With my body I shadow my son
from light too bright
for him now. The dark of my breasts
and shoulders settles
over him, warm, a blanket.
My hands in the light above him turn
light slowly—allowing it,
receiving the quick
rhythm of its windy slant
as it brims in the window glass, west.
My hands slow and soften it. In the past,
countless times, I've nursed
the children like this—magic,
Brook likes to call it, and Paul
explains that light
massage will align
the blood's hemoglobin, carrying oxygen
and calm deep within.
I accept that, and the light,
without comment. I do nothing here
but let my hands remember
Brook as a newborn
for whom each breath of alien
air in his lungs is fire,

fire and fear of separation. As if
he's naked, dressed only in the wet,
cheesy stuff that was, before
his birth, the interior
and greasy swaddling of my body,
now again he is the sprawl
of flesh and tearful
spirit too delicate to touch directly.
The fontanel—how it pulsed.
Drawn too near the fire,
he must knit—must learn to be
complete, and so my hands hover
over, they trace tendrils in the light
air—they soar and curl,
lowering gently, finally
to a touch that translates, *I'm here,*
we are both safe,
we have not perished.
Lulled, replenished, he floats
beneath my hands—and I remember
how I was drawn to the table
just yesterday as sun fell—
alone with the simple
wood where, whole and entire,

hours earlier, we had gathered
for food. Then I closed
my eyes, put
my hands on the wood,
into the sun—surprised to feel,
element by element, the table
releasing itself—wood back
to the grove of walnut trees, nails
to original ore, ore
to earth. Hands that cut
and planed, that dug and smelted,
that guided the torque
and turn of metal
into nail, that polished sawn
wood to a finish like silk—
these clasped and unclasped
down the long line of women and men
who made them, the table
now sun and rain
in the trees, the table now wind
in a sift of stars
over continents and oceans—the table
released, shimmering, and brought back,
light, my hands on the table

pulling the light slowly in
as one draws breath, holds it
briefly, savors, releases, and moves on.
But I could not move from there.
I could not—as if I were
a child who believed an angel
had slipped her hands inside my own
and shone there. There was a power,
and the power made
heat channel through my hands.
I let myself feel the power,
keeping still, holding firm,
hollowing, hallowing
space, that light might come
and dwell there, heal
and be. I left med school to find
what power there was in keeping still.
And so, I could not move from there—
but did, of course. There was the kiln
and the family to tend—
the very things
I say the power came by, took it.
I let the light go—for it was a table
there beneath my hands, not my son in pain,

coming calm. And it takes, dear God,
this pain of his to make me see
how my dream returns,
healing—how it has not
swerved from
its quiet insistence and summons.
I hear my mother say, *Angel.*
I see her, lit and torn,
bringing salve, and Jennie
spilling water, her hands bright
around a glass—and now suddenly,
the seam of the dream's inside
out, the moment transparent.
No one, no lie, comes between.
This is—my dream
spinning tangibly here.
Light, what do you want? I whisper.
Brook murmurs, *Stay with me,*
stay. The light in the window wavers.
I hear Comfort take a scale
boldly, six notes, and seven—
the last one turning, home.
But I know someone, someone
missing, wants me. Wants me to come.

Jennie

Leaving, *now?* She must be crazy, and I tell her so. Hasn't she labored, worked for months, she and the others, turning pots and drying them, carefully stacking them in the kiln? Isn't it her kiln, and temperamental— is she not more responsible? There are: yes: shifts assigned, and each woman takes her turn at the vigil. The kiln will get tended. But firing's the peak of the process she prides herself on, beginning to end—she would leave that? Oh, yes: go to our father—who never loved anyone: always there were women around him, and he built houses: around them. Go to him—but now? Why now? I watch her closely. She flushes. Her eyes burn, two banked fires: between us: a felt space, that firebreak between angers. And though I know I will not have my way with her, I can see in her flush what my words do not admit to: that I may have: have: I have hurt her.

I pause, aware of Lila: pleased with me: pleased. My rage at Sarah slackens. In the pause, Brook defends her. *I'm OK*, he whispers. A few minutes more, and he's saying, *Take the gold leaves to Grampa when you go.* And still I'm waiting for Sarah to answer me, watching Lila warily, thinking: my God, I did this for her, I spoke the words for her: for my mother. I feel the smoldering inside her: heat pressing through her skin and cotton, like a scorch from an iron: yellowing. Never mind. I'm waiting for Sarah to answer me. Her silence hangs on a hinge as exactly as a door. Then she says, *When Kate comes, you'll know what to do.* Sarah mysterious, maddening—as if nothing I'd said: not earlier, with our arms around each other: not now, at odds in a room of dust and light: could be true enough to matter.

So that's how it is, says Lila as Sarah leaves us, in her voice the tone she substitutes for anger: dismay. Then she croons to Brook about cocoa. I remember her with cookies still warm, bread and jam. The need to please, the need to smooth over, to sweeten. Rules have been broken, an implicit order denied. Food will fix us. I sit down with Brook: in my charge now: and prop his arm on a pillow. We'll play Scrabble, I tell him. We'll look at stills and photographs culled from my work, signed and put in a sequence, just as they'd be in a book. But first we'll wait: for cocoa, I tell him, strict in my expectations. A family of rules, a family of ruses that would hold back chaos, sweetening—that's what we are, and from such families comes at least one child who would make something. In this family, two. From the low table by the sofa, I lift a bowl: graceful: sturdy clay so thin walled it glows, ruddy in its glaze. I turn the bowl over—unsigned. *Work is its own signature,* Sarah said once. But I challenged her—*You are the work. Sign it: claim it!* And Sarah? *I'd as soon sign a child.*

I feel pressure in my throat: familiar darkness. I feel curtains blown, and wind. I hear a rustle of sheets—I feel them kicked down to the foot of the bed. I don't want to. I don't want to remember the men and my struggles: against them: for love. I find Brook's burn to stare at. I come fully back to this room: Sarah's house. I hear wind in the shagbarks. Lila's spoon in the pan of milk. Brook asks about my photographs. *I'll get them now*, I say as Lila comes to us with cocoa: two cups. None for me? Never mind. The phone rings. I feel a pressure in my throat, crossing to answer the phone in Sarah's house, Sarah gone to her father, forsaking all others. *This is Sarah's house*, I say quietly, waiting to hear the voice that will ask for Sarah.

In the pause: listening: I hear what I have no time or space to hear, moving in my fluid life, event to event, frame to frame, lover to lover. No time to hear a daughter: prodigal in her energy: howl as she's pulled from the gape between my thighs, and the cord cut instantly, as I'd asked. No time to hear my daughter: unrecognized: howling as she's given over. I see Sarah's outstretched hands. I close my eyes tightly. I won't cry. I hear the baby wailing. I hear Sarah murmuring, and my own voice: urgent: calling for pain-killer, for darkness—and that darkness granted me, who heard a daughter howling and failed to inquire: signing her over: if the lie would hold, if it would keep our lives separate. I who have never failed since to inquire, whenever my work: sought after: goes public, *What if it should fail*—not good enough—*what if it should fail?* You're too hard on yourself, friends say—who do not know how often I seek darkness and the anonymity of flesh: moving quickly, murmuring into the wind and rumpled sheets, forgetful.

The voice asks for Sarah. It's Paul. But Sarah's face has faded from the room: white: bone white. No sound but wind. I want the chill of that wind to rush right through his skin and hurt him. I want to hurt him. I don't want him here. On the sofa Lila snuggles Brook, her broad breasts his cushion. He sips his cocoa, and Lila hers. *There's nothing wrong here*, I would tell him—this man who knows my cowardice. That I cried out for darkness. That I promised: promised: I will tell Kate when she's ten: well then, in five more years, in Taos, a family vacation. But instead, I kept silent: the sting of the camera my truth. Paul is saying he's seen Stephen at the hospice, watched him breathe: long lapses, no breath left—then ragged gasps, rapid panting. *That means he's dying.* Good, I think: but my *good* hurts me. *Sarah's nearly there*, I tell him. And here? How is it here, without Sarah? On the sofa they sip cocoa. I feel my ribs. I press hard. Hunger hurts. Then I lie to them all: to the cocoa that comforts, to the phone that inquires, to the room where my father breathes: white: bone white. I lie to Sarah, nearly with him. *Here? Here, things are fine.*

Lila

I will sit with this child long
as need be, his head held close,
milk and sun mingled in our cups.
Miracles come—sudden
shifts, as in my garden, so warm
this October, earlier in the Indian days,
that sprays of azalea opened lavender,
tender and lush, and the gulls flew
out of their bodies, changed. They were
flashes of light.
                    That's not possible,
Jennie says to the phone, tossing back
her tumble of hair. Who is she talking to,
so secretly, a lover? An old anger
stirs. An old remorse. I remember
wineglasses, and my pain, quick
as a cantlet of glass on the floor—
that sliver of glass, that raw glint
the vacuum missed, pass after pass,
but foot found, up late and restless,
bare.
            I remember the childhood nights
your sleep turned fitful, Jennie,
and I went to you, quieting
feverish dreams, wiping tears—
but there were too many afternoons
I'd put you, angry, down for naps—
I'd hear you moving, secret in your bed,
and hurry in, move your hands,
smell your fingers—saying,
That part of you is secret. Don't touch.

And just once, for shame I pulled
the covers from you, rigid—
and drew your legs up by the ankles,
drew them up from the bed
where you lay still, on your back,
lifting you as I would an infant
to spread a diaper under. Like that,
I held you, your nightdress slipping,
privates bare. You'll hurt yourself,
I said—so young, too young for this.
You didn't hear me then—won't,
now. It's too silent between us.

Oh, don't tell me about the breaking
of a woman—how men do it.

Haven't I had a hand in it, too?

Jennie

I feel Lila's eyes, her steady gaze. If I turn, her look will absorb me. If I turn, I will take the cocoa from her and drink. My stomach churns. A sudden energy: pressing upward: sends me down the stairs in a hurry, down the hall, where I close the door—quietly. I would not, even now, have her know. I crouch on the floor. Arms against cold porcelain. Arms balanced against the rim of it: white: bone white. Head bowed over the bowl. Far back, back where the flesh of the mouth is tender, I move the tip of my finger back and forth. Dry heaves. Sour spit. I gag. I try to retch. I spit. I spit her out. I spit her out of my body. Hunger is mine. I press hard. Hunger hurts.

A daughter comes home to be recognized: empty-handed. The family wants it that way. She is safer without her camera on her, without her photographs of cities and their streets. What has the family to do with *Fuck you* and *No Hang Out Here* drizzled on concrete stoops in Day-Glo colors, with peeling paint and garbage cans banged in by street fights, with the git-down-time of prostitutes and pimps? Sweep it all out of sight. A man curls up under cardboard. A man goes stiff with cold on a steam vent, sleeping. A woman sucks the pap of a whiskey pint dry and calls it breakfast. A man unwraps the bandage on his foot, finding the only vein he has fit for a needle. A fruit stall opens. Dirty air films the grapes. The cabbages are stacked like skulls back home in the killing fields. Here the killing goes slower. Even the avocado, soft and dark at its pit, knows the festering heart of the human wish to die. *You could nuke that hell-hole tomorrow and do nine dollars worth of damage,* my father said once. I spit him out of my body, too—with each shudder of my body, more free.

A wave of grief fills my gut, and I ride it out, remembering how he kept me out on the Sound to watch a summer squall come up river: how the boat pitched in the troughs of the waves—first the town spire, then houses, docks and pilings going dim as the wind and rising dark made for us: sails luffing like bedsheets, rain white on the water upriver, making for us— and when it hit, he pulled over the sail he had lowered just in time. In that shelter of canvas, wet, we rode it out—*alive*, he insisted, *alive*. Here now: on the cold tile: no black water rushing white, no visible strain of wind to lash shrouds and stays, my body shelters its secrets and its pain. It tastes salt. It hears the roar of wind, blood pounding in its skull. I stand back from it, watching. With me, I realize: also watching from the threshold of the opened door: is Comfort. How like Sarah she looks, repeating dumbly in her flesh her mother's need to serve another's pain. *Are you all right?* she asks. Her voice is tremulous, small.

I shake my head: no. I rise, I rinse my face. She hands me a towel and says nothing. I leave her by the door, walking rapidly down to Brook's room. My hands are hot: my cheeks flushed, feverish. In my suitcase, among scarves and smooth cottons, I come across the sudden gift of a necklace: cool to touch: the chill of Connecticut and October on cowrie shells and coins sewn on a wide collar of black burlap. The shells are ivory, cream— they have the sheen of wet silk. I remember they were once used as money: simple sheltering husks turned to a sort of power. The coins themselves are gentle squares with rounded corners, thin, gray as pewter. The tigers on them: rampant in a silent roar: resemble gargoyles. Their tails curl up their spines like question marks turned backward. They must wonder: Where is the power—where is the gift of power fled to? A very female property, this necklace I could offer to Comfort for her complicity: *Don't tell*.

I hold the shells and coins against my cheek. So this is what you are. Now Comfort shyly knocks: two raps, the syllables of my name: or hers. She brings me tea, she brings me essence of mint and honey in a cup. She smiles, and: fearless woman: I let myself sit with her on the bed, saying nothing. I sip the tea, savoring. *This is wonderful,* I tell her, surprised to feel grateful, humble. She has freckled cheeks from too much sun, like her father, the displaced father of my child, his freckled body not mine to count on. *Kate will like that,* Comfort says, touching the necklace jumbled in my lap. *Are you better?* Please God, I nod: don't let me use the necklace: bought on a street no woman should walk alone: as bribe. For I could give it to anyone: mother or daughter: saying, *He spoiled everything.* Saying, *Never mind. Love the necklace. Love me.*

Now Comfort takes my cup and leaves me hidden in a world of thought. The door clicks, and I follow my father out of this house, where he's been living: sober: with Sarah and her family. I am thirty-two, unloved and restless. I track him, dark coming on: suspicious about the afternoons he hunts for Indian graves, coming home only as birches tilt up between satellites and stars, late for dinner. I bend east over stone walls, down a ridge. His words I carry with me, sour on my tongue: *I hunt what no one owns, no one marries, no one wants.* I find him huddled on a mound of stone grown over with moss and running cedar. He doesn't try to hide the bottle. He mutters. How the ground is cold: corruptible: sacred. How they sat the dead down naked on the ground, without weapons or food, chanting, then mounded the stones over: bone against earth, stone against earth, years of rain softly following stone and bone into the earth. I make him look me in the eye. *You want to die, and you can't. You want to hurt yourself: and the rest of us: don't.*

Freeze-frame it: *don't:* but he laughs, calling wind and snow and rain down to lash him: if that's what it takes: pinned down by the naked will of it. I left him then to stumble back alone, telling no one. *Let him drink—he only hurts himself*—that's what I thought: that's what we all think, numb or indifferent, giving to the methods of tortured relation civilized names: tea and toast, a drink before dinner, dinner. I remember my father's ambition. I remember white houses with well-cut architraves and windows—over the lintels the pineapple of hospitality: an urn of death, egg and dart. And the dinners: bone china, white linen, roasts of meat. Wine in the glasses—never enough! After the first drink, not a thousand are enough. Never mind the pain. *That means he's dying.* "Good," I said. "It's time."

I listen to these words: no sound but wind. In the background: fluent: I hear women's voices. Laughter, footsteps quickening, the bump of Comfort's cello up the stairs. I hear my mother's name called out, and pleasure in the greeting of that cry. I stiffen. Bone by bone, I begin to shiver: contracting: as if I were my father's mortal chill. *I have never had a mother.* I whisper the words, stunned by their simplicity. *I never had a mother.* Overhead, a light ripple of sound, applause. That would be bread from the oven. Or Phoebe, home from dance class: born to a ready audience, her family: so far: undiminished by death or shocks of repeated absence—her family expanded to receive these women. Potters who can touch emptiness at the core and turn it: firm it: fire it, and find for it a use. Oh, *Take me,* I want to cry. Within me the cold contracts, the dead lie down: unmothered. I bend over: head on my knees: and rock myself: finally able to, weeping. How I wanted to be separate! And I am: instead: this need to be taken in.

Upstairs, before a fresh fire, Sam, the fat brown dog, stretches out. Phoebe feeds him crusts and butter. Comfort tunes her cello, the room whirs with words. The room is a litter of talk and tea things, cups and plates with their leavings of jam and crumbs and crusts. Brook is tucked into the corner of a sofa with a book. Here and there, as I cross the room, come greetings. But I'm on my way to the kitchen, where I see Lila at the table: alone: watching through the window the last birds in the feeder, the last edge of light. She doesn't see me coming. She lifts her hand and rubs her forehead, smoothing out the lines—and I can see how she was once, herself a daughter, selfish and afraid: ready to bargain for her own salvation: my life if you will love me. But how can I love her? Once I challenged Sarah: *Tell me*. And she, returning the challenge, said, *Think of a moment: one that was shining. Just then, you loved her.* When I could remember none: none shining: she lent me one of hers. Lila outside in the moon-bright yard, up late in her negligee, turning and turning behind the stockade fence and ivy: dancing: full and light, pregnant with me, lifting her thin gown and turning, barefoot on the shadows of leaves and the lit night grass. Now I draw near to her, who once danced her body and mine out into a night too beautiful to sleep. She is still Sarah's mother more than mine. I draw near, and she looks up, uncertain. *How are* you? she replies, giving back my question. *Hungry*, I say softly, *hungry*.

She has me sit at the chopping board to mince parsley. You do this: she directs me: I'll get the kettle. Phoebe dances in, taking parsley as I chop it. She fists it into the butter bowl, messy. In a moment, she's off to another distraction. Outside, the light goes from rose to smoke and blue. I feel the weight of the necklace in my sweater. Lila comes with two cups. *That Phoebe*, she says to the parsley on the floor, but sits down, quiet, still lost in her own smoke and blue. Then she looks up. We could meet, two angels dancing on the prick of a pin, light flashing from our feet. We could say, *Kate's not coming home:* or, *She's coming.* We could say, *Stephen's dying:* or, *He's not.* We could say, *Ease this pain.* But, taking a fork, she begins to work the parsley into the butter, blending it quickly. Phoebe is now, she tells me, not much older than Bart was. Blending, she begins to remember: without reproach: for was I even born? She tells me how it was with her that night. How she pressed his little trousers, starched his shirt. How she ironed. How the heat of the shirt felt to hands grown cool from his wet skin. How she washed and dressed him, how she combed his bright hair and sat with him in the dark of the house, his coffin open to the stars. I shiver. The pathos of the stars makes me know: or think I know: that she is lying: taking truth and breaking it: how she'd have had it: her way. She butters bread, and I watch the knife stroke the surface, covering it thickly with butter. Over years of white tables: full of her loss and her emptiness: she passes me bread, and I take it. I eat and feel the necklace weight my wool, disparate shells and coins on a black ground strung. In the background: far back: women's voices. I listen to their voices, and to Lila's, surprised that the lie she tells turns: slowly: into my willingness to receive it. This is her gift. What she can give me. I take the lie gently. In my pocket: cool to touch: coiled: cool as a root: there is this necklace.

Kate

I lift wine from my knapsack, clear sun in green glass,
and savor its sour breath, like my own

after a bad night's tumble—I could spill it,
slow as rain on the sallow buff and ocher of a shell,

its color ripening in the wet relief of wine. I could remember
Sarah's good-night, god-bless kiss, so light it's invisible,

energy that savors of fire, what fire promises.

In wine I could remember my own room, stars on the ceiling,
a welter of sea glass, my prom dress

black and silky. My belly tightens. No matter how happy
you have been, it says, *Be careful, be angry.*

What is a girl with two mothers?
                    Drunk, he told me.

I drink wine straight from the bottle, so fast it runnels
down my neck, slides cold between my breasts—

why hadn't I known it, felt it?

I remember the road unwinding to Taos. Just then
I had Sarah to myself, without pots to fire or children—

and Jennie, her wild hair down her back, a chaos of books
in the trunk, her camera, a Katsina we'd bought secretly

for Sarah, blue corn for the Corn Mother (should we meet her).
And from the Keres this question—central to their culture—

now I hear it, fact raw in my memory, another shock—
Who is your mother?

Mother understood by the Laguna (Jennie said) as work
unsullied by weakness, by doubt—

Mom stared at Jennie, then back to the road—barren
mesa, Navajo *kaya,* sheep and silhouette so occasional

they only marked how broad the emptiness was, the expanse
of twilight a smear left where an upswell of rock crest

pressed sky—that land her mood. But Jennie at the wheel
talked on, words from books, the speed of the car

compelled by the speed of idea. Too much talk. Too much
silence beneath talk that hurt like pulled muscle.

I drink. I watch my fire tug up from its wick of wood
into a day going plum and rust, going blood.

The wine sinks in my gut. And God yes, I want to slip my hand
inside and bring it up, blood on my fingers—

I want to taste it, mark my face, take wine, and drink—
but the wine is spilled, the wine

is drunk—and the blood won't come, it won't.

Light sinks, and I follow it, borne on a drive of wind,
on a length of fetch, to the edge.

I could dive, break a hole in the sea, release my breath
into deep black water, and never tell them—sweet

fool, I'd be *glide* and *breathe* and *float*,

I'd be the thrill of pain in my nipples—dying and alive,
stinging with salt glaze, stung,

floating in fire—cold fire.

I look overhead. Stars blur in the wind, stars burn
on the ceiling. I don't know.

I hold myself still. Home is my body, breath
my own—to do with what I will. Oh, but somewhere,

deeper down, feel it,

Sarah's teaching me water, to lie back in the watery
silk of cattails, in the flow of sky and a tree's green billow

upside down in the ripples of the pond,
in the redwing's nest turned spiral and meander,

each thing around me softening, passive to a wider will.

But if I don't want that wider will,
                                    what then?

Sarah

Before I enter, at the door
alone and secret, I pause
for balance at the threshold,
and for breath.
I breathe slowly, a scale
of muted notes that rise, and fall,
and rise. Smells, immaculate
and sterile, tinged with
salt and medicine and oil,
swell, recede.
How bare it is—window, chair,
and the bed where my father
sleeps, his body a faint
ridge of white beneath
the cover, his head
tilted, mouth
open, hardly a stir of air
going in, out.
And the hole that is his mouth
(that used to blow a kiss, or swear
or grin, telling stories)
that liminal hollow of breath
barely felt,
is the naught that draws me, here.

I release the will to be home,
fire rising in the kiln.
I release my will to find Kate,
or stay with Brook. To hold them.
Through tears I wait until
again I can enter
what I know of water and sun,
letting myself be drawn
beyond own will—to a movement
that, silent,
seems flame—
flame and emptiness, and promise.
I let disperse
all will but this—
I have come to be with my father.
This man who has made me burn.
This man. My father.
I cross the room,
open the window, find a pitcher
for water. I've brought
yellow chrysanthemums,
as acrid and bright
as the lie I could tell for comfort—
but won't—

that Lila and Jennie come tomorrow.
They won't, and the yellow
bough of maple, leaves
about to curl at the edges,
is from only Brook.
Quietly: to resist the lie.
Quietly: to accept
what the moment, infinitive, gives.
I run water, let it
splash about the sink.
The water chills, the water grieves.
I want water softly to wake
this man who has gone from his family
so often, that the sound
of water running, gone by,
says more aptly,
Father—father, good-bye,
than anything Jennie might say,
or Lila, too numb, too hurt.
I think of the flat stone I've kept
in my studio, a round
O in its center where water sank,
drop by drop, and hollowed.
And for the will to receive

the power of water
into the stone of my grief,
without asking to achieve
anything by my being here,
but being here,
for that will-be-done
I ask. *Your father*
wears his motives on his sleeve—
my mother's voice weaves
in and out of the leaves, as if
alive only by wanting to relive
what's as bitter
as the smell of these blowsy flowers,
heavy-heads
that shudder as I move
the pitcher over to his bedside.
I laugh softly at myself—
voices in flowers? Absurd.
That's better. A raspy whisper
meets my laugh.
A slow turn of his head.
The news of my death has been
greatly exaggerated.
Aha, I say. *Mark Twain—*

let us now quote famous men—
I know the game, a favorite
of his, and it's my turn.
Let me think, I say, but I can't.
Though he turns his head
toward me, he can't lift it.
Beside his mouth, a white
smear has dried, the medicine
he drinks to soothe, to coat,
to cloak the ravaged
linings burned by acid,
blood and gall,
and alcohol,
years of it, his recent
abstinence too late.
All I can think of is Twain
again, *Do not bring your dog*,
the first line in a monologue
on funerals and etiquette—
just his wit. A special
defiance he'd call
giving necessity the guise,
graceful or raucous, of rigamarole.
But then I see his eyes.

They hold mine steadily,
a careful stealth,
as if to inquire
beneath anything said openly
whether I know what he knows.
What I see takes my breath—
there's death
in his eyes, a fact the social poise
of his manner denies—the gesture
of a hand graciously
extended—still the host of the party
who cares, if not to please,
then somehow to amuse.
I take his hand and hold on—
not too tightly,
though I want him to say
it, let death
be spoken between us, energy
summoned consciously, agon or koan,
claimed, used—*This is mine*—
and let go of, the gift given.
And not this guarded non sequitur,
this detour—the truth
of the moment deemed improper.

No matter what death I'd opt
for, myself—this is his
to shape and honor, or not—
and so love, that profound
courtesy, has me respond
simply, *How are you?*
Tired, he whispers. *Tired.*
Then he winks. The rake returns.
I'm what they say, in and out.
He likes the phrase.
He croons it as he sinks
into the lull drugs make
of his body, medicine
his merciful angel, his retreat.
In and out, the quick
trip he always promised, into
the gin mill and out—just one.
I hear the surface pattern
of excuse, *in and out,* the taboo
rhythm of the afternoon affair, a sunrise
swim—a slantwise
permission for pleasure and guilt,
wry refreshment, and no
sense of the pattern his pain makes.

How can I tell him what he ought
to do, or feel, or be? Again,
his mouth falls open,
his breath spins wide, spins down.
He's lonely as a tunnel.
I go over to the sink. Breathing quietly,
I let water run. If I am to enter
the unknown pattern each moment
gives, at least I can
enter also the comfort of water
as it takes the shape of whatever
form surrounds it briefly.
I cup water to my face,
rinse its outline, bone and skin.
I feel how lightly
water makes sorrow's trace,
not a touch unless
touch means lightly
letting go. The room's sublittoral
as a shell, clean as salt.
My father's hand flutters open,
grasps air, shuts.
Eyes closed, wincing hard—now only
this pain left to believe in.

I sit down, now finally
with him. He kicks the cover
fretfully, like a child who would
bully illness. And he says,
though he doesn't open his eyes
or give any sign
that he feels my hand on his,
After all this, what do I know?
Out the window, far
from the misted shore, an ease
of sea horn, low,
gives itself to the sea.
Again, low. And in the pause
between two notes, I whisper
to him. How every night as a child
I looked for the light
late—beneath his door—
or opened the front
door—wishing him home with us.
If he wants the release
this shyly offered truth tries
to give, I trust—I feel
I must trust—him to take it.
Does he? I can't tell. But the yellow

flowers deepen
as if they might transmit more
light from sources beyond
what we know. I feel our lonely
honesty as if it were color.
And suddenly I'm met
by the single most vivid memory
I have of him alone—in the stern
of his craft, the line
lightly held as he waits
for wind that rises with the sun,
wind that settles east, where
the lighthouse is a bright
needle, and the wind threads
round—a ripple,
ripples—and now wind takes the ready
modesty of the sail—
and yes, the joyous
shout he gives as he goes
running with the morning wind,
one with that motion.
I feel my pain, and his, subside.
Wind and sun come to meet my father,
and I hold that brightness close.

The door opens, and a nurse comes
with a basin, a towel folded
beneath it, and a smile
that wants to be tactful, but isn't.
She wants me to leave while
she washes him. I begin to defer—
but here's my father curled
away like a child from the cold,
from the dark, from the blind
sources of pain without name.
I'll be glad to do it, I say
quickly. *I'm his daughter.*
And the guile of that non sequitur
combines with the docile
truth of the offer to surprise her.
I'll just turn him,
she replies, handing over the towel
and the oil, her look reminiscent
of Lila's disapproval.
I try to reassure her,
filling the basin, testing the water
for warmth—efficient.
She turns him from one side
to the other, careful

to tilt his head back. She spoons
chalky stuff down his throat.
He swallows, submissive,
though he rucks up his mouth,
the folds of skin
beneath his jaw so loose
they crease like a ruche.
She checks the level of his urine
in the plastic bag, undoes
tubes taped tightly to his wrist,
and leaves. Acrid,
the odor of urine weaves
about us. *I hate the smell of piss,*
he whispers. *I'm afraid.*
I shiver—this is what it means
to be naked, exposed
utterly, the first and last
pulse of each primitive
moment a death, a death, a death,
and still the ruse
of dignity, though it grows thin,
thinner, finally transparent.
Carefully I place my hand
around the curve of his chin,

my cheek to his forehead,
pressing gently. *Afraid?*
I ask him to think of the sea
he loved to glimpse
just ahead as the path of beach plum
narrowed in the dunes, the rim
of the tide line rising,
the presage of a fine sail
felt in the frail
billow of a web held
taut in the salt wind
that skiffs up the steep sand—
and once again I'm a child
with my father's enthusiasm
for the sun to buoy me,
and nothing harsh has come
into this paradise—
though it will,
and how shall I say, *Be grateful*,
no matter what unmeasured
passion flames or chills?—
so I rock him until the rousing
sea slides still,
and he sleeps in the measure of my arms,

neither father nor lover.
He slips past my hands
into an eclipse of consciousness
too deep for me,
past the image of the sea
I gave him, for courage,
to follow. I loosen
the knot of the blue hospital gown
and slip my hand inside,
his skin dry as paper.
His flesh feels hot. He shivers
and sighs with the fire inside
him—an emptiness
in the shape of a flame, a whisper
of the intensity of his solitude.
My role here is to tend—
what little I know transferred
to the work of tenderness
this work is. Forgive us
(I murmur) this
day (and yesterday's doors, hard
edges that opened, closed,
and kept us separate). I massage
his shoulders lightly—remember

the basin, now cool, and the oil.
I resume the pattern of tasks—
nothing special,
renewing the water, soaking the cloth
and smoothing it, more quiet
than warm breath, across
the gray hair of an armpit,
down fallen muscle—
wiping smoothly the rough
burl of an elbow, a slow progress
down the bend of the back's
long bone, his skin a bisque
yellow and gray—the slack cheeks
of his buttocks, and the crease
between them, his legs,
the long plainsong
of thighs and calves, the cradlesong
of belly and scrotum, and the idle
penis, an afterthought,
limp as a curl.
My hands take on the heat
of him, traveling the thin lathe
of the ribs, over heartbeat
and slack breath—the unsung

history of his soul somehow held
in the hover of breath I feel
moving across my hand
as I wipe the stain of medicine
from his chin. Where his skin
blazes from the pressure of the bed,
I use the oil, then cover
and sit with him,
my hand over the one of his he still
holds in a fist. I remember
my childhood Angel,
abundantly light, abundantly color.
Light gathers and turns in my hand,
over the burning ground,
here—light
brims in the room, the curtain
fills, the Angel
fits her hand to mine.
In the quiet light,
brimming, I feel
how round and clear the moment,
how fragile—light
reconciled with light, only this moment
world without beginning, or end. And amen.

Kate

I shiver outside the bedroom windows—and by dim night light
and shadow find them. Phoebe snuck out of her room

to sleep with Brook, Comfort asleep with her homework sprawled
on the covers. And here I am—

doing what Sarah would want, looking in on the little ones—
held here, kept here, kept.

What is a girl with two mothers? I remember my father at night,
salt smell of his sweat, lifting me and spinning me

overhead, prelude to being carried off to bed. Too many
mothers, too many. They give, then take away,

my fathers. I draw near the window to my room.

Gramma's there. I close my eyes, remembering,
and I see beneath silk soft as a bird's wing, folded

in a drawer, the photo of a boy who looks like me, my own
likeness concealed beneath silk

I can't imagine Gramma parting for Grampa, for any lover—
but so she must have. I didn't hear her coming.

He was special, she whispered, lifting the boy from my hand,
you, so like him, special, too.

Of all the windows, hers I stand at longest, as if her feeling
for Grampa, unfinished, might be touched awake.

But she sleeps on.
I clamber up the deck, unsteady on my feet—no railing—

and see them inside on sofas, in sleeping bags, resting—
these women whose kiln weekends I loved,

the pace of the house revved up—stoking, sleeping, eating,
song and celebration. I stiffen. I don't see Sarah,

though we made songs, we sang together, sang to excess, voices
hoarse with laughter—all that nonsense

sky high—the firefly, lullaby years with Sarah
fled, my mother a saucy song the wind sucks off my tongue.

> *the moon is in the basement*
> *the yard is dark and still*
> *the sun is in my belly*
> *do you hear the whipporwill?*

And Jennie—what does she tell me? Nothing, no word, none—
she comes into my head in a coat too big for her, jostled,

homeless, a bum's rush of a woman, and just like that, coat
turns kimono, silk, and it rinses between my fingers,

it puddles into the cradle of a drawer. Never mind.

Time to mud over the firebox—my specialty.
They need me at home, at the kiln. They need me to seal

the door swiftly with wads of rolled clay, old newspaper,
and a slip taupe as suede. Each October,

this firing—and so close to my birthday that when the kiln,
cooled a week, is opened and the pots taken out,

it's my day, Hallowe'en, and Sarah gives me the pick of the kiln.
Trick or treat, she could say. *Trick or treat.*

Oh, but these are my hands—rough with working mainsail and jib,
shroud and stay—my skin burned by a sheet's easing

fast. *Live with it.* These are my hands.

Sarah

I cut the headlights of the car
and pull near the stone wall.
Walk in the rest of the way,
something tells me, I don't know why.
Overhead, Orion
tilts west into spires of cedar,
stars on a black background
strewn. Unseen,
the moon, newborn, is drawn
along up there in its groove
of curved space, its power
dark and naked, so tangible
I can smell it in the ground
damp with cold,
in the shriven stalks and pods
of milkweed stripped for winter,
along the branches of swamp maple.
Just to be in darkness, alive,
with my father's smell still on my skin,
quickens the silence that sieves
through me. I draw near the kiln shed.
Fire shoots in tongues out the chimney,
licking—any higher,
it would glaze the unseen moon.

In the darkness, voices.
Low and tremulous, intense—
and pauses that raise silence an octave,
then blaze.
Kate's voice—Kate!—and Jennie.
I hesitate. I should not go near.
In a rush (no time to prepare
ahead, ask to receive,
knock for opening, know
what to feel, what to do)
I'm jealous.
What joy I felt with my father
goes—in its place
an unfamiliar dread.
Kate and Jennie together.
Jealous? I would not feel *less*
or, seeking to deprive,
feel deprived. But jealous, yes,
jealous. I don't want to lose
her, left outside
the circle of their burning ground,
hidden by darkness, and God, so tired—
a weariness so profound
I stumble up the hill. My house

is black and still,
no yellow oblongs of light
let down on the lawn from the windows.
When I turn to look back at the kiln,
I see dark outlines,
women with light
flung round their headstrong lives—
and nothing I can make, no bowl
so vulnerably open
it hurts,
will appease or atone.
I will have to go down there.
I hear my father's raspy voice.
After all this, what do I know?
My hands are hot, that I know.
I lift them to my face,
and they burn.
Live openly, they tell me,
openly. Oh, but
I wanted Kate to be my daughter.
I wanted the lie
to hold us in a hoard of grace
and never go. And somehow,
I will have to tell her this.

Jennie

Stoking, I see her coming: *Good,* I think—composed, her arms braced about her in the cold. I shake my head. She said Kate would come, and she was right. But did she smell ahead: in the wind: the brassy stench of wine from her daughter's throat? Or see broken clay? each pot taken from the shelf of unfired pots and winged, Kate's arm a clean stroke, swinging roundly. The clay gave way so easily: as earlier Rachel had, sent off by Kate's assurance: *I know what to do.* From the set of her jaw, and a glance my way, I know she knows Sarah's come. She works fast, dipping sheets of newspaper into the slip, slapping it over the bricks and wads of chinking. She doesn't look up from her work. *Keep stoking,* she calls. I stop. Stoking's her work. And hasn't she, taking the fuel of wine into her body, stoked enough? *You asked for it,* earlier I told her. *To give him wine is to ask for it. For you to drink is to ask for it.* Sarah glances about, taking the kiln shed in. She hasn't spoken. She can't know yet how Kate has said to me, *You must. Must go to Grampa with me. Tomorrow.* "That's not possible," earlier I said to the phone. Suddenly, I see what will happen here. Like me, Sarah will relent and do what she doesn't want to, yielding—too guilty to resist.

Sarah

I see the stiffness in her spine,
and I feel it. Spoiled,
the ware in the kiln will
be spoiled, the door
mudded up too soon, the ware
let to bake too cool
in a reducing atmosphere,
smoke dark haze.
She has the skill—she knows
what she is doing. This is bald
defiance. This is willful,
and despite the burn
in my stomach—*it's right*,
this roiled blaze, her anger
as close-hauled
as the fire's muted roar.
What were pots, outside the kiln,
are now a maze
of blank shards left to litter
shelf and ground—all but one
bowl broken. Odd and lone,
left out of the destruction,
spared. An oversight? A mute
beseeching. And a dare.

See me. See me, it says—my God,
like Bart, like Bart
entangled in the mooring line
of my father's sunfish,
without any sound or outcry
that would carry over
the seawall,
the hedge, the lawn—
the whole house turned away
from his agony, his fear.
See me—for a while, treading water,
his body heavier
for the prized box of stones
and shells in the pouch of his jacket,
no one awake enough to hear water swish
through those stones. Into my throat
the dream rises: live openly:
here we are,
one turn more on the spiral,
the circle rising, full of light.
Not too late to hear Kate's mute cry of pain
break on the air like a startled
question, or to match it with my own.
I fix on the bowl Kate left intact—

too narrow in the foot,
its round hollow too perfect,
surface too mute.
And suddenly, rising
without knowing what it is—
as once a silhouette of wings
from the cliff's edge rose,
swept by an updraft
into ripples of sun,
rising with wings—
I take the nearest tool
in hand, and for Kate,
for Jennie, for my mother,
and for me—full
in the power that embodies
perfect vision, full
in the power that forgives us
our failures to hold it
embodied, still—
I break it open to the light.
What I feel is heartbeat,
heartbeat—*here we are*.
I hew to the moment,
trembling. And I wait.

Kate

I hear a crack of iron loud on clay and look up—
tears startle into my eyes, and fear I didn't know I felt

when I broke the pots eases. I remember watching a snake
slough its own tight skin, wet ripple of long muscle,

fresh strike of sun, then flick! She has finished my work.
She's allowed it.
                    A corner of newsprint furls,
catching fire, and I slap it back, wet with slurry.

Inside the kiln, smoke cools like a stain on the tight skin
of the pots. Oh, but let it stop with me,

let the suffering stop! I will not, in my own flesh,
carry secrets.

The corner of newsprint furls, I pull it away, chink

by chink prying firebrick loose, letting air burst through,
working fast. I wipe my hands, toward Sarah and Jennie

turning, and I remember the necklace they gave me in Taos,

how it fell cool on my skin, right as rain. Jennie watched,
Sarah fastened it. I felt her hands on my shoulders

turn me round, turn me toward her,
turning me as if I were, and willingly, my own new world

gently spinning against her hand.

Sun burned our shadows into hard earth—on a lengthening slant
the three of us etched on a sand hard as rock.

I test the ground beneath my feet, as if it were a bridge
over dark rifts, remembering what Grampa said, too maudlin drunk

to mean it. *Blame me.* Instead, I say (all I can say)
(to begin with),
                    How's Grampa?

Jennie

Once, women in Seattle, walking arm-in-arm in protest against lies, murmured *mmmmm,* one sound as they walked. In the quiet that falls after Sarah's blow, her bowl collapsing, I hear *mmmmm.* "How's Grampa?" I watch Kate. I watch Sarah's face. Our father's dying. So much else to say to Kate, she will want to hold back what's raw and new. *Don't do it,* I think. *Tell her now.* Something's new—I feel it in the broken clay. Coming back, faint white, light circles the kiln shed, swelling. *Should I come live with you—would you want me?* In my head: far back: voices rise. *Do what has been given to do,* Sarah said once. I'm still the girl she spoke to: and not. I watch Kate: and Sarah: both moving nearer to each other and to me. Before Sarah can meet Kate's question, I hear Kate say into the humming quiet, into the upbringing dawn, her voice rising, *I have something to tell you, listen . . .*

Lila's Dream

No longer sheltering in the family and its things, I lift out of my body
as once, in Kill Devil Hills, I watched a cloud of geese lift from the winter
    wetlands,
one body, a lake rising into the sky

He put his hands inside my coat, his hands were hungry, they found my
    breasts
and the hard, sweet currants of my nipples
He breathed wind into the hollows of my neck, his breath warm and damp
    through the wool

No longer sheltering in the body's blueprints, its branches and roots,
in a gasp I leap the last synapse
across which each impulse has traveled faithfully, to and from the light on
    the surface of the Sound,

and the roof of this house is less than the question I shaped as a child
from a stir of fear or desire
                       What is death

A mother lifts the top from the small house of dolls, and a child peers in,
    omniscient
Tiny pans are on the stove, the beds are made, the tiny teapot, no larger
    than a nut, is singing,
and the child begins to hum,
rearranging the house given into her power

The question slips with the linens into the cupboards, folding into the scent
    of lavender and mint,
the linens tiny squares, hardly big enough to staunch a scratch

Someone, no longer alive, is hovering, each breath in, breath out
that last release that fills, and empties,
the house, taking everything with it
                          brick shingle window door

And I see the space that spins within things, light and the silence of light
        finding horizon
in each facet of screen, each spoon, each cup

What is it like, leaving the body? I have wandered out of the house at night
as wind threshed stars from high, back-lit billows of mist
The wind rises, and falls, and rises

It is like following my own breath
without the wedding of the body, without the gravity of earth

Between walls of wind, I see a woman and a man standing in grass that
        used to be a lawn
I know there was a house there once, because lilac and shade trees and over
        there
a clump of green thick with lilies
rises next to the cement and brick foundation

And she asks, pointing to the space between lilac and the line of boxbush,
        there a family played croquet,
that was a smooth course of lawn the family kept for evening games
and there were tables with cloths the wind lifted at the corners, were there
        not

From up here in the wind, the shore is a crescent horn worn down to
    eclipse
by the sea's endless power of recollection
The Sound is a broken line of white where it washes the rocks and enters
    the whorl of the sea snail's house
A bottle breaks against green rocks

I hear footsteps down the hall, a door opening and closing like the sea
My face is wet with tears

Sarah, it will be Sarah, the Sound humming, *chiva chiva chiva* rising from
    shagbark and maple,
awakening the heart from its ancient sleep

And I know what she will tell me, oh I know